The Return of the
HEADLESS
HORSEMAN

The Return of the
HEADLESS
HORSEMAN

MATT CHRISTOPHER

Illustrated by James McLaughlin

THE WESTMINSTER PRESS
Philadelphia

Book Design by Alice Derr

First edition

Published by The Westminster Press®
Philadelphia, Pennsylvania

PRINTED IN THE UNITED STATES OF AMERICA
9 8 7 6 5 4 3 2 1

Library of Congress Cataloging in Publication Data

Christopher, Matt.
  The return of the headless horseman.

SUMMARY: Two boys on a fishing expedition are
surprised by a headless horseman, believed to be the
ghost of a nineteenth-century horse thief.
  [1. Mystery and detective stories. 2. Ghosts—
Fiction] I. Title.
PZ7.C4577Re   [Fic]   81–21936
ISBN 0–664–32690–0   AACR2

*To
Martin, Margaret,
Michael, and Melanie*

One

In the stillness of the night,
While even shadows slept;
He rode.

THE SOUND of pounding hooves in the middle of the night? Steve Russell couldn't believe it.

"Jim!" he whispered, tensed. "I thought you and I would be the only ones awake at this hour! Do you hear that?"

"Yeah," answered Jim Dano, his friend. "A horse. And running like crazy."

"Right. Super-crazy, if you ask me."

They were fishing off the edge of the bank of Cedar Bay. A three-quarter moon peered down at them like a sleepy eye.

Steve looked over his shoulder toward the road from where the sound of a galloping horse was coming. Trees stood like tall, dark sentinels. Branches stuck out like dangling arms. That alone made the hairs stiffen on Steve's arms. The sound of the running horse made the atmosphere spookier.

The boys were allowed to stay up so late only because Jim was visiting Steve and wanted to do some night fishing. Grandpa George, Steve's father's father, had been fishing with them, but he had left to go to bed over an hour ago. Grandpa lived in a basement apartment of the Russells' large, two-story house which stood some sixty feet to their left. Next to the house was a stable and a corral where they kept their four riding horses.

Won't Grandpa George be sorry he didn't stay up later and see what we've seen? Steve thought, excitement bubbling in him.

Now Steve glanced at Jim, wondering how he had reacted to the sound of the horse's pounding hooves. Jim and he had been school buddies before Jim and his family moved to Utica, where Jim's father had a new job as a math teacher. This was the first time Jim had visited Steve since they had moved. Now Jim's eyes were wide with wonder.

Suddenly the boys saw the horse. It was galloping along the road, from left to right, its long, fat tail waving like a pennant.

Steve shuddered. "Jim, look!" he whispered. "That rider! He doesn't have a head!" Stunned, he almost let go of the rod he was holding.

What is this—a dream? he asked himself. He inhaled deeply, then exhaled.

A few seconds later horse and rider were far down the road. Out of sight.

"Jim!" Chills rippled along Steve's spine. "Did—did you see what I saw?"

Jim seemed frozen. Only his lips moved. "A rider without a head!"

"Right! So I wasn't seeing things. It was real!"

"It sure was!"

Steve looked down the road again. His hands holding the long, slim rod trembled. "Let's reel in," he said, tensed. "This is going to be a scoop for Dad. Wait till old David D. Davidson the Third hears about this!"

"David D. Davidson the Third?" Jim echoed. "Who's he?"

They stood up and began to wind their reels as fast as their fingers could fly.

"The big-shot owner of the *City Daily*," Steve

answered hastily. "He's been trying to buy out Dad for six months. He wants to hog the newspapers for himself."

It was a cutthroat business, Steve's father had told him. Just like a lot of businesses. But David D. Davidson III ranked at the top of the list. A real hog, Steve said to himself.

At last he saw his hook spring out of the water. The worm was still on it. He reeled the line in slowly, caught the hook, removed the bait, and laid the rod on the ground.

Seconds later Jim finished reeling in his line.

"Let's leave our rods here," Steve said. "Come on!"

They bolted through the semidarkness along a path that Steve had covered so many times he could run it blindfolded.

They reached the house and raced up the long flight of steps two at a time to the porch deck. A soft-yellow light was on.

Sorry, Dad, Steve thought. But this is a scoop. You'll thank me when I tell you. I know you will.

He pushed open the unlocked back door and stumbled inside. He caught his balance, ran across the kitchen floor. His footsteps sounded like an army on the run.

Maybe the noise was enough to wake his father up, Steve thought. Maybe it was enough to waken his mother, too. And Grandpa.

He heard Jim behind him, heard the kitchen door slam shut. There was no light on in the house, but the moon shining in through the uncovered windows lighted the room enough so he could run through it without bumping into anything.

He ran down the hall, past the open staircase. Breathless, he paused in front of his parents' bedroom door.

"You'd think we made enough noise to wake up an army," Steve said, panting. "Man, when they sleep, they *sleep.*"

He was about to knock, and Jim caught his arm.

"Steve! Listen!"

Steve listened. Those pounding hooves again!

"He's coming back!" Steve cried. "I don't get it!"

They ran back to the kitchen, looked out the

window toward the road. They saw nothing except the trees, heard nothing except their own breathing.

"He's gone." Steve's heart pounded. He looked at Jim. Then stared at him and grabbed his shoulders. "Hey, man! You okay? You're white as a sheet!"

Jim closed his eyes, took a deep breath. Then he nodded his head. "I'm okay."

"You sure?"

"Yeah."

"You're just scared, right?"

"Yeah. Right."

"Well, so am I," Steve admitted. "Brace up, and come on."

They returned to the bedroom door. Steve's father was emerging from the room, tying the belt of his bathrobe, rubbing his eyes.

"Dad!" Steve cried. "Have we got a scoop for you! A real hot one, Dad!"

"Oh, no! Haven't you guys gone to bed yet?" his father demanded.

To bed yet? Is that the kind of response I get? Steve said to himself. Wait'll you hear what we would have missed if we *had* gone to bed!

"Dad, Jim and I—" He faltered. His tongue was getting twisted.

"Take it easy," his father cautioned calmly. "You and Jim what?"

"We saw a horse and rider," Steve said, trying hard to control himself. "And the rider—oh, man, Dad! You won't believe this."

Mr. Russell turned to Jim and frowned. "What's he trying to say, Jim?"

Jim cleared his throat. "He's trying to say that we saw a rider on a horse, Mr. Russell. And the rider didn't have a head."

Two

In long black cape—like Death,
He plunged through the night,
Fearless and mighty.

"NOW JUST a minute, boys," Mr. Russell said, holding up his hand like a traffic cop. "It's night. And it's dark out there. What sounded like a running horse to you—"

"It *was* a running horse, Dad," Steve cut in. "We saw it. And we saw the rider."

A light was turned on in the room. Steve saw his mother put on a robe and come around the bed and into the hall to join them.

She squinted against the light. "Where were you two when you heard this horse and saw the rider?" she wanted to know.

There you go, Steve thought, the third degree. She won't believe us, either.

"Fishing from the bank," he answered sullenly.

Her blue eyes shifted from one boy to the other. "Go to bed," she said. "Both of you. You're starting to see things."

"Ma!" Steve cried. "It's true! We both saw them!" He glanced at his father. "You want to save your newspaper, don't you, Dad? What better news can you get than this?"

"The newspaper is no concern of yours, Steve," his father said firmly. "It's my problem. I'll handle it."

Mrs. Russell looked at him. "Robert, it's mine, too," she declared. "It's *our* problem."

"Well, okay, it's our problem." He turned to Steve. "Someday I expect you to take over the business, son. But that'll be a long time, yet. You're still too young to worry about our problems."

Maybe I am, Steve thought. But if I have a chance to help you now, Dad, I have to do it now, he wanted to say. This can't wait till I get older. What if the *City Daily* got onto it first?

The *City Daily* had almost twice the circulation of his dad's newspaper. It was published every day, whereas the *Courier* was published

only twice a week, on Tuesdays and Saturdays. The *Courier* covered mostly local news. It had excellent sports coverage, crime too, with credit going to the police whenever they arrested law offenders. And credit went to citizens who did a service to the community.

Robert Russell wrote the editorials himself, and he pulled no punches. Because of his honesty his paper had won an award almost every year since it started. And five times he had won the Western New York Newspaper Award for excellence in editorial writing.

Steve was proud of his father. It was his wish to be a newspaperman when he grew up, to be like his dad. Well, half like him, anyway, he told himself. Nobody could ever be as good as his father.

His mother stifled a yawn. "Look, boys," she said, putting one hand on Steve's shoulder, the other on Jim's, "Dad and I don't mean to be disrespectful. But you know as well as I do that a thing like a horse carrying a rider without a head is stuff from stories years and years ago. Washington Irving wrote 'The Legend of Sleepy Hollow' many years ago on that theme. What you thought you heard, and what you thought you saw, must have been some sound from back up in those woods, mixed with your imagination." She chuckled and her eyes brightened as she seemed to recall something that had happened to her. "I'll never forget when—"

"Sorry, Ma," Steve cut in. He clutched Jim's arm. "Come on, Jim. I guess we woke them up for nothing."

They started up the hall. Mr. Russell shouted, "Steve! Come back here!"

Steve hesitated. He looked back at his father glumly. "What's the use, Dad? Neither one of you believes what we told you."

"Just a minute, now," his father said calmly, moving toward the boys. "Your mother and I would like to get this thing straightened out before you run off with *your* heads loose on your shoulders. It is just possible, you know, that there was a sound like a running horse coming down the road. But it could've been an airplane that you heard. Probably a helicopter from the army air base. They fly around here quite a lot."

"Of course," said Steve's mother, smiling and folding her hands in front of her. "That's a more logical explanation. And what you thought you saw were really shadows. Isn't there a wind blowing out there a little?"

"Just a little," Steve admitted. "But it wasn't the sound of a helicopter we heard. And those weren't shadows we saw. It was the real thing."

His mother unfolded her hands and held one up. "Wait. Where was Grandpa George all this time? Wasn't he with you?"

"Yes. Earlier. Then he went to bed." A grin spread across Steve's mouth as a thought occurred to him. "Wait'll he hears about this in the morning!"

Mr. Russell smiled. He laid a hand on Steve's shoulder. "Don't get upset about it, son," he said softly. "Your mother mentioned 'The Legend of Sleepy Hollow,' but maybe one of you —or both—once heard about an incident that was supposed to have happened close by here, about a man named Cyrus Cornfield, a horse thief who lived, and died, about a hundred and fifty years ago. Maybe that's what was in the back of your minds when you saw what you thought you saw. Right?"

Steve frowned. "I never heard of it," he said.

"I did," Jim said. His face lighted up. "He

was caught and hanged."

Mr. Russell nodded. "That's right. And his head was cut off."

Mrs. Russell uttered a soft cry and gaped at him. "Why did they do such a horrible thing? Wasn't hanging him enough?"

Mr. Russell shrugged. "The story goes that he would not die, so one of the mob did it."

"Ugh," said Mrs. Russell, making a face.

Steve looked hard into his father's eyes. He had never heard of the story. If he had, he couldn't remember it. Had it anything to do with what he had seen?

He got a funny feeling inside his bones that maybe it had.

He looked at Jim, and Jim looked at him. Did Jim have that feeling, too? But Jim didn't say anything, and neither did Steve.

He turned back to his father. "Then you won't take our word for it," he said calmly. "You don't think it's worth even one small paragraph in our paper."

Mr. Russell patted him on the shoulder and smiled. "It would be a big joke on us, son," he said. "David D. Davidson the Third would have a laugh that would be heard all over the county. No, I'd say forget it. It's pretty late. It's already past midnight. Hit the sack, both of you. And keep that story about the headless horseman to yourselves. Okay?"

Steve tightened his lips. Sure, Dad, he thought. We wouldn't want to embarrass you for the world. And, if David D. Davidson the Third scoops you, we'll just let it go.

"Come on, Jim," he said, whirling away. "Let's hit the sack."

Three

On and on, with echoing hoofbeats,
The horse sped, its tail flying,
Its eyes like flame.

STEVE HEARD his mother calling him in the morning. There was urgency in her voice.

"I'll be right down, Ma!" he answered. What now? he wondered. What was so important this early in the morning?

He washed, got dressed, and hurried downstairs. Jim was already at the table, having breakfast with Mr. and Mrs. Russell.

"What's up, Ma?" Steve asked.

His mother picked up a part of the newspaper lying next to her coffee cup.

"You've made your father and me eat crow for breakfast, that's what," she said. "Take a look at this."

He stared at a picture that was featured on

the front page of the *City Daily*. It was a drawing of a horse and rider, done by a member of the newspaper staff. And the rider was headless.

Across the top of the page the headline read: HEADLESS HORSEMAN RETURNS!

Steve read the headline out loud, staring wide-eyed. Then he looked at the drawing. It was of a horse running just as he had remembered seeing it. And the rider was headless.

There it was. Proof. He stared at his mother and father. Anger reddened his face.

"There you go," he cried, pointing at it. "There it is. Right on the front page. But you wouldn't believe us, would you? No. What do we know? We're just kids."

"All right. We're sorry," his father apologized. "We're very sorry we took you so lightly."

Steve let himself cool off. What was that old saying about spilt milk? "That's okay, Dad. Forget it. What does that article say?"

Mr. Russell looked away from him.

It's hard to forgive you, Dad, Steve thought. But, if I were in your place and you in mine, maybe I would not have believed you either.

It *was* weird, he had to admit.

"It says that at least five people saw the horse and the headless rider," his father said. "And they weren't all together, either. One person saw them near the corner of Melon Lane and Perry Road. All the others saw the horse and rider on Perry Road. But all of them were a quarter to a half a mile away from each other when the horse raced by them. Here. Read it for yourself."

He shoved the paper toward Steve, and Steve started to read the article.

" 'Could it really be Cyrus Cornfield, the horse thief who was caught and hanged and then had his head cut off a hundred and fifty years ago?' " he read. " 'Records in this newspaper's files tell us that Cyrus lost his life—and his head—on June 28, exactly a hundred and fifty years ago today.

" 'The hanging took place near the old Markson homestead, located about a mile east from the Perry Road–Rockefeller Lane crossing. The Markson homestead was burned down in 1945, when it was bought by the town and a garage was built on the lot to store the town's trucks.

" 'This isn't the first time the famous—or infamous—horse thief was seen riding his horse down Perry Road,' " Steve continued reading. " 'The first time was in 1860. He was also reported to have been seen in 1890 and 1925, which means that Cyrus has no set pattern as to when he takes his nighttime rides.' "

Steve looked up from the paper. His fingers were trembling.

"I wonder if anybody ever tried to follow him," he said.

"Several have," replied his father. "With no success. The horse always turned off the road somewhere past the Markson homestead and vanished into the woods."

Steve finished the article and laid the paper back on the table.

"One thing I would like to know, Dad," he said, gazing seriously at his father. "Would you have put out a special edition this morning if you had believed Jim and me?"

His father looked at him intently. He rose from his chair and tugged on his belt. "I would have had it out even *before* that greedy old bat, Davidson, did," he said bluntly. "I'm very sorry, son. I wish I had believed you boys. I guess I just couldn't make myself believe that in this day and age something like that could really happen."

Mr. Russell got his suit coat from a closet. He put it on. "I'd better go," he said. "I'm sure I'll hear about this the minute I walk into the *Courier* building. Rusty Mitchell, my elevator man, will be the first one to throw it up to me."

He leaned over and kissed his wife. Then he shook hands with Steve and Jim, and left.

Four

On he rode, blending with the night,
While animals scurried, and
Bats shrieked.

AT NOONTIME, Grandpa George stepped
into the kitchen while Steve, Jim, and Mrs.
Russell were having lunch. He greeted them
jovially and said something about having fed
the horses. Then he pulled out a chair, sat
down, and wanted to know what all the fuss
was about late last night.

Steve and Jim took turns telling him, saying
that they wished he had stayed out there fishing
with them. He would have seen the headless
horseman then, too, and surely Steve's parents
would believe him.

A merry twinkle came into Grandpa's gray
eyes as he grabbed one of the cut sandwiches
from the lazy Susan. "So that's what all the

commotion was about, eh?" he said, and chuckled. "Cyrus Cornfield rides again."

Steve looked at him. "You believe us, don't you, Grandpa?"

"Sure I believe you," the old man replied gruffly. "If you said you saw it, you saw it." He sank his dentures into the sandwich and started chewing.

"Well, Jim and I saw it, all right," Steve said, not knowing whether to believe his grandfather or not, "and that's good enough for us." His mind went spinning off as he munched on a peanut-butter sandwich. "Ma," he said after a while, "would Dad have anything in his newspaper morgue about Cyrus Cornfield?"

"I doubt it," she said. "Your father has been publishing the newspaper only twenty-two years. That thing about Cyrus Cornfield happened a hundred and fifty years ago. I don't remember your father's ever publishing an article about Cornfield. Do you, Grandpa George?"

"Never," said Grandpa.

Steve ran a hand across his mouth. "I'd just like to see if there is any more about that guy I can find out."

"There could be. And if you can find out anything else that D. D. Davidson hasn't printed, your father will appreciate it, I'm sure." She cleared her throat. "I talked with him on the phone this morning. He didn't sound very happy."

Steve frowned. "What happened?"

"Four of his big, regular advertisers called in and asked how he expected to keep circulation up with poor reporting."

"Oh, no!" Steve's hands gripping the sandwich froze in midair. "I'll bet Dad's sick, Ma."

"Of course he is. But it'll take more than that to knock your father out of the business."

"I know. But if four big advertisers complained this morning, there might be more this afternoon. And tomorrow."

She sighed. "Let's not talk about it anymore. You're too young. You might as well forget about this Cyrus Cornfield."

"There you go again. Too young. Well, I just can't forget about it, Ma," he said emphatically. "I want to help Dad." He took another bite of his sandwich and chewed on it a while. "You think they'd let Jim and me in the morgue at the *City Daily*?"

"Why not?" cut in Grandpa George. "Sure they will, even if you are the son of its competitor."

Steve smiled. "Thanks, Grandpa."

After lunch he got pencil and paper and then he and Jim biked to the office of the *City Daily*. As Grandpa George had figured, the boys were allowed into the newspaper's morgue to search for back issues of the paper for articles about the headless horseman.

Remembering the dates when the horseman had appeared, Steve looked for and found the 1925 issue. He read the whole article. Then he looked for the 1890 issue. But the paper didn't go back beyond 1914, the year it was started, so he had to be satisfied with what he read in the 1925 copy. The most significant news he found in the article was that the headless horseman had always appeared *twice* within a twenty-four-hour period.

He put his notes in his pocket, thanked the girl who had given him and Jim permission to go into the morgue, and left.

They had hardly gotten out the door when a

boy about Steve's age suddenly stepped in front of them.

Of all the guys to meet! Steve thought, not too pleasantly.

"Well, well! If it isn't Mr. Russell!" the boy exclaimed, glancing with amusement at Steve, then at Jim, and back at Steve. "Can I take one guess what you guys were doing here in *our* morgue?"

Steve had always tried to like David D. Davidson IV. They went to the same school. But it was hard to like a guy who seemed to think he was superior to everybody else.

"You don't have to guess," he said.

"Well, I will. You were researching Cyrus Cornfield and his return as the headless horseman. Right?"

"Clever," said Steve, not impressed. "Your dad had quite a scoop."

David smiled. "You weren't surprised, were you?"

Suddenly a movement beyond David caught Steve's eye. He looked past the boy's shoulder and saw a tall, red-haired youth stepping across the aisle between a cluster of busy desks. The youth knocked on a glass-paneled door, then

37

disappeared into the office.

Steve frowned. "Is Marcus Robard working here?"

"Yes," said David. "He's covering sports for us. Mainly horses."

"Oh."

"I guess you should know him. He lives near you."

"Yes. His father owns the farm down the road from us. We ride our horses together quite often."

"Hey, that's great. Well, I've got to push on," David said. He stepped aside to let Steve and Jim pass by. "See you guys. Okay?"

"Right," said Steve. "Take care. And thanks for letting us use the morgue."

"Hey! What are morgues for, right?" David's laughter trailed after the boys as they walked down the hall and out of the building.

"He a friend of yours?" Jim asked blandly as they got on their bikes and pedaled down the street toward home.

"No, I wouldn't say a friend. We just go to the same school. I guess you weren't impressed with him, were you?"

"Let's say I don't think I'd care to have him on my team, no matter what kind of sport it is," Jim said.

"What I figured," Steve replied.

He wasn't surprised. He couldn't see Jim teaming up with David D. Davidson IV, either.

Five

Once a thief, lawless and bold,
Stealing horses from honest men
For pieces of silver.

A KNOCK on the door startled Steve. He was lying on his bed, fully clothed. His hands were folded behind his head. The tiny lamp on the nightstand beside his bed was on. The alarm clock beside it read 10:30.

"It's open!" he said.

It was probably his mother. Or father. Some last-minute advice about the ride. Maybe they had reversed their decision. They had talked about it further and decided it was too risky. Yeah, that was probably it. He and Jim had better not attempt anything "foolhardy." That was the word his father had used about the boys' plan of following the headless horseman if it rode again that night.

The door opened. A head came into view. "Hi. I hope I didn't wake you."

"Hi, Jim," Steve said. "No, you didn't." He rolled over on his side. "Hungry? Feel like raiding the frig?"

"No. Nothing like that."

Jim was fully dressed, too. But something was bothering him. Steve could tell.

"What is it, then?" Steve looked at him curiously.

Jim seemed fidgety. "I've been thinking about tonight. I don't think we should do it."

Steve bolted to his elbow. "What? You chickening out?"

Jim took a deep breath, blew it out.

"Look," said Steve, "if you don't want to come along, okay. I'll go by myself. I can handle it." He rolled over onto his back again.

How do you like that? he thought. He had depended on Jim. Two bodies were better than one, he figured. Jim could hold the camera and the flashlight while he handled the horse. Some friend you are, Jim, old boy.

"Please don't be mad," apologized Jim. "I just think—"

"Never mind," Steve cut in. "You're right. It's risky. Maybe we'd get killed chasing something that isn't supposed to exist. Go ahead. Hit the sack. I'll see you in the morning. If I'm not dead."

"Steve, I really wish you would think it over."

Steve looked at him. "Did my parents send you up here? Did they ask you to do this?"

Jim just stared at him. That look, Steve thought. Jim didn't have to admit anything. That look told it all.

"What I figured," said Steve. Anger sparked inside him. "Well, go back and tell them I'm not a little kid anymore. And that they promised. Go back and remind them of that, too. Okay?"

He rolled over onto his stomach, shut his eyes and turned his face away from Jim. Scram, Jim, he wanted to say. I don't need your help. I don't need anyone's help. I'll handle this alone.

He heard the door open and then close. A moment later a tear appeared in one eye, oozed through his eyelashes, and rolled down his cheek. The pillow absorbed it.

At eleven thirty that night Steve snapped off the light and walked out of his room, carrying his shoes.

All the lights were off in the house. He didn't hear a sound except his own movements.

Someone was in the kitchen. He could see the person's outline. Someone sitting at the table.

He paused at the bottom of the steps, tensed. "Who's that?" he whispered.

"Me. Jim." The answer came back in a whisper.

Steve frowned. "I thought you—"

Jim got up. "I changed my mind," he interrupted. "Come on. I've been waiting for you."

Steve didn't move. He didn't know what to think. This was a surprise—Jim's changing his mind.

"Come on!" Jim insisted. "A guy can change his mind, can't he? Get your shoes on. We don't want to get out there too late, man."

Steve smiled. His heart lightened. Everything he had thought about Jim while lying up there on the bed vanished like smoke.

"All right," he said.

He put on his shoes, tied the laces. Then he got the camera and the flashlight, and they left

the house as silently as cats.

They went to the garage, their shadows moving like weird wraiths beside them. The garage door was open. They stepped inside. A horse whinnied quietly.

"Easy, Fire," said Steve. "It's me."

He heard the horse blow through her nostrils and felt elated. He had ridden Fire, a chestnut mare, dozens of times, more often than he had ridden the others. He and Fire were great friends.

Steve had sneaked out and saddled the horse just before bedtime. Now he mounted Fire, settled himself on the saddle, and pushed his feet into the stirrups. He checked the coil of rope looped over the saddle horn. He wasn't sure he would use it. But it was there—in case.

Then he helped Jim mount behind him. "Don't drop the camera," he warned. The camera. It could turn out to be a very valuable instrument tonight.

"Don't worry," Jim assured him. "I've got both—the camera and the flashlight."

They waited.

"If that article's right, he should be riding by again," Steve said softly. "It said that he always appeared twice within a twenty-four-hour period. That means he'll show up again."

"And if he doesn't?"

"He doesn't, that's all. Then we'll hit the sack."

You're still scared, aren't you, Jim? Steve wanted to say. You're probably wishing he *won't* show up.

Well, not me. I wish he does. It'll be a chance for me—for us—to find out if that headless horseman is real or a phony.

Either way, it'll be a story for my father. And maybe it'll help hold some of those advertisers who threatened to cancel.

That's the real reason I've got to do this, Jim, his thoughts ran on. To help my father. To help him save his business. He never says much about it in front of me. But I've heard snatches of his conversations with my mother, and I've added them up, and I have come up with a lousy score.

His business is hurting, Jim. I know it is. And if I can help him, I will. I've got to.

Suddenly a rapid, thumping sound came from the south end of the road. *Tata-rum. Tata-*

rum. Tata-rum. The pounding hooves of a horse!

"There it is!" Steve cried. He untied the rope that had kept Fire tethered to a post, and held firmly onto the reins. "Just hold it a second, Fire," he whispered, crouched low on the horse's back like a jockey. "Just one second."

The second passed. And another . . . and another . . .

Then he saw it. Like a swiftly moving shadow.

Six

Eyes that pierced the night like steel,
All-seeing, yet themselves not
Visible.

HORSE AND RIDER seemed to travel even faster as they rode past the entrance to the driveway. Steve could see them clearly now.

And the rider was headless!

Oh, man! No matter what he had thought about the rider before, seeing him again sent shivers through Steve.

"Hang on, Jim!" he cried.

Feeling Jim's arms circle his waist and tighten around it, Steve jabbed Fire in the ribs with his heels, and they were off.

Fire broke from the garage like a racehorse leaving the starting gate at a track. She bounded up the blacktopped driveway, her hooves pounding.

At the entrance, Steve tugged on the right rein and led Fire onto Perry Road. About a hundred yards ahead they could see the galloping form of the headless horseman.

Little by little they gained ground. "Go, Fire, go!" Steve urged.

Suddenly something captured his attention.

"Jim, look!" he cried softly. "Don't those shoulders look as if they've turned a little? As if he's looking back at us? Now he's turned away again."

"You're right, Steve. It seemed as if he *did* look back at us."

"Maybe he's got eyes in his shoulders," Steve said, kidding.

Jim laughed. "Yeah."

The laugh wasn't genuine. I know a real laugh when I hear it, Steve thought. Jim's was forced. He is still scared. Still uptight about going on this venture.

I should have gone without him, Steve told himself. He might turn out to be a burden. So now I'll have to contend with him and maybe lose sight of the headless horseman for good.

Baloney.

The gap between them and the headless rider

seemed to have closed to about fifty yards when suddenly the horse ahead turned off the road. Steve saw that it had arrived at the county garage—had turned off into the driveway.

"Keep your eyes peeled, Jim!" Steve said. "We don't want to lose him!"

Shortly afterward they reached the building, too. Steve yanked lightly on the left rein and Fire turned off into the spacious driveway. Up ahead, dark woods faced them.

The headless horseman was out of sight.

Steve yanked on the reins, pulling Fire to a halt. He listened intently for a sound to come from within those woods—the sound of a horse's hooves. But he heard only the sleepy calling of birds. The hoot of an owl.

A chill rippled up his spine. "I'll be darned, Jim," he whispered. "He's vanished!"

"Think we ought to go back?" Jim said.

Steve looked at him, not too surprised. "You mean give up?"

Jim shrugged. "Well, he's gone, isn't he? We don't hear him."

Coward! Darn you, Jim, you're a coward! Steve felt like telling him.

He kept his control. "You figure, then, that

he's a phantom?" he asked, turning farther around in the saddle to get a better look at Jim's face.

"I don't know. But if those articles in the newspapers were telling the truth, what else can a guy think?"

"Yeah, what else can a guy think?" Steve echoed. He turned away, hiding his disgust.

"Forget it," said Jim. "Forget what I said."

"Look, if you want to go back, I'll take you back," Steve offered bluntly.

Jim shook his head. "No. If you're going to try to follow his trail, I'll stay with you."

"You mean that? Don't say it if you don't mean it."

"Yes, I mean that," Jim said tersely. "Let's go."

A broad smile crossed Steve's face. "All right! Go, Fire!" he cried, and snapped the reins against the horse's neck. "This ride isn't over yet!"

They plunged into the dark woods, but they had to slow down because of the darker shadows, the closer-knit trees.

"There's a tunnel near here," said Steve. "The entrance of an old railroad tunnel. We won't be able to find it easily, because they took the tracks away a long time ago."

They ducked under an overhanging branch of a tree.

"That isn't all," Steve went on. "Robbers used to hide in there. Even nowadays, when a guy escapes from jail, that's one of the first places the cops look."

"Have you seen it?" Jim asked.

"Yeah. And I've been in it. But for just a little way."

He remembered that he was about nine when he and his father had hiked into the woods in search of the tunnel. His father had taken pictures of it and of bats clinging to the walls inside and had written an article about it.

Man, he thought. That seems like a hundred years ago.

They came to the base of the mountain. The mouth of the tunnel was somewhere here, he remembered. He led Fire along the steep slope, taking care to avoid fallen trees, stumps.

"Where in heck is it?" he exclaimed. "Darn! I'll bet anything that that headless rider's gone into it!"

"Don't you think whoever followed him before tried the tunnel, too?" Jim said.

"The article said they had," Steve admitted. "But, still, he disappeared, didn't he? If he's a phantom, I'll buy that. But, if he isn't—" He paused, and then pointed straight ahead. "There it is!" he cried. "The mouth of the tunnel!"

"Shall I turn on the flashlight?" Jim asked.

"Better. We'll have to see where we're going."

Jim switched on the flashlight and they entered the tunnel.

"Oh, wow!" Jim breathed, flashing the light on the black, scarred walls and ceiling. "Look at those bats!"

Steve looked, and felt a tremble pierce through him. "Just shine it straight ahead," he said.

They continued on. Steve began to feel a chill gnawing at his skin. He shivered.

Maybe this is crazy, he thought. Maybe Jim was right. Maybe we should turn around and go back. And maybe Mom was right. Maybe that rider, that headless horseman, was just in our imagination. Maybe we just thought we saw him. Maybe, maybe.

You're just looking for an excuse to turn around and go back, he told himself. Who is acting like a coward now, Steve, old friend?

"Want to keep going?" he whispered.

"You're the chief," Jim replied. "Whatever you want to do, I'll do."

Sure. You would say that now, Steve thought.

They ventured deeper and deeper into the tunnel. I don't know, Steve said to himself. He began to have doubts. Had the headless horseman really come this way?

A cry burst from him as Fire's head dropped, and her front legs lost their footing. Steve heard the horse splash into water, and he fell in headfirst too.

He heard a scream just before he disappeared into murky depths. Terror seized him. This is it, he thought. I'm going to die.

Seven

Phantom? Or was he real?
Was his horse genuine,
Or was it a phantom, too?

THE WATER was ice cold. But Steve's out-stretched hands touched rock. The pool had a solid bottom.

And it was clear. A light shining from beneath him blazed a cone-shaped path through the crystal-pure water.

A second shock hit him. The light could only mean one thing—Jim had dropped the flashlight!

Questions flooded his mind. Where is Jim? Can he swim? Is he hurt?

Steve forgot about dying. He was still alive. Still able to act. He swam to the flashlight, scooped it up, and shot for the surface. His lungs ached for air. The moment his head cleared the water he opened his mouth and sucked in a lungful.

"Jim!" he yelled. "Jim!" His desperate cries echoed against the walls of the tunnel.

He shone the flashlight around as he treaded water. Fire was scrambling out, stepping up onto the flat ledge at the side of the pool, her muscles bristling like rope under her flat, velvet coat. For just a couple of seconds more Steve kept the light on the horse to help her see her way. Then a cry burst from close behind him. He spun.

"Jim!" he said, and he almost panicked.

Jim was struggling desperately to keep his head above water. He was puffing hard. Then his head sank below the surface. Terror gripped Steve again as he swam toward his friend. *Don't drown, Jim! Oh, God, please don't let him drown!*

He reached Jim, put an arm around his waist, and paddled hard toward the side of the pool. Torn with fear, he kept yelling, "Kick, paddle, Jim! Kick, paddle! Keep your head up!"

He could see that Jim was trying, trying hard to kick and paddle and keep his head above water. Fortunately, thought Steve, they hadn't

far to go. He hated to think what might happen if safety was any farther away.

They reached the edge of the pool. Jim, gasping for breath, climbed up and stood on the wide ledge. Steve climbed up and stood beside him, shining the light on him. Breathing hard. Feeling thankful they had come out of this alive.

Steve's teeth chattered. His cold, wet clothes clung to him as if they had been dipped in ice.

He remembered the camera. Oh, no! he thought. It must be in the pool!

He shone the light down into the water, moved it around. Then he saw it.

"I've got to get that camera, Jim!" he cried. He handed Jim the flashlight, then dove into the pool. He grabbed the camera and brought it to the surface. Climbing back up to the ledge beside Jim, he shivered with cold and wetness.

"What lousy luck," he said grimly. "The film's probably ruined. Camera too."

Jim remained silent, his knees shaking, his shoulders hunched.

"L-let's take off our clothes and wring them out," Steve said. "They'll dry quicker. And we might not be as cold."

They took off their clothes, squeezed all the water they could out of them, then put them back on.

Steve shone the light over the pool. "N-not bigger than a home pool," he observed. "And a lot shallower."

"Yeah. But still t-too deep for me," Jim replied.

"You never did learn to swim, did you?" said Steve, noticing the embarrassment in Jim's voice.

"How can you when your parents are afraid of the water?" Jim asked.

Yeah, thought Steve. I guess I'm lucky. Both Mom and Dad love the water. Love to swim.

"Well, what shall we do? Go back, or keep on?"

"After what we've been through?" Jim shrugged. "Can anything be worse than falling into that cold water? I say keep on."

Steve stuck out his hand, and Jim slapped it.

"Right on!" Steve said.

Eight

He laughed at pursuit,
Knowing his pursuers would give up
The search.

JIM MOUNTED Fire first, and Steve handed the camera and flashlight to him. Then he mounted Fire in front of Jim, and they rode on.

The ledge was about five feet wide, and it was perhaps the same width on the other side, Steve assumed. Beyond the pool the tunnel narrowed to a width of about fifteen feet.

Now and then Steve heard Jim's teeth chatter. He tried to keep his own firmly together, but now and then they chattered, too.

Good thing Fire came out of the ordeal without getting hurt, he thought thankfully. And, being a strong animal with a thick hide, maybe she won't catch a cold, either.

But what about Jim and me? Steve asked himself. We're thin-skinned, shivering like a couple of scared rabbits. What's to keep us from catching a cold? Or bronchitis? Or pneumonia?

Doubt about continuing on began to gnaw at him again. Was this making sense, risking a serious illness for something they might not be able to find, anyway? Was it really so important —tracking down a headless horseman who might not be headless at all?

Steve yanked on the reins. "Whoa, Fire," he said.

"What's the matter now?" Jim wanted to know.

Steve looked around at him. "I'm giving it another thought," he said. "We're cold. Half freezing. And we're not sure we'll ever catch up with whatever that thing is we're chasing. Shall we go on or not? I'll leave it up to you."

"Leave it up to me?" Jim echoed. "Fine thing! I thought you were doing this to help save your father's newspaper!"

Steve stared off into the dark spaces. "Yeah, I was," he admitted.

"Was? What do you mean 'was'? Who's talking about backing out now?"

Steve blushed. Jim was right. Who was talking about backing out now? And look at what Jim had been through. He might have drowned.

And I thought *he* was chicken, Steve told himself. He's making me eat my words.

"Okay," he said. "Let's—"

"Steve, listen!" Jim's sudden whisper startled him.

Steve listened. And far off in the distance he could hear the almost inaudible sound of running hooves.

"A horse!" he exclaimed.

Jim wrapped his arms around Steve's waist. "Let's get going!" he cried.

Steve jabbed his heels against Fire's ribs. The horse responded, jerking ahead and then maintaining a slightly faster but steady pace.

"If that headless rider is a phantom, I'm R2-D2," Steve said.

But if he is no phantom, who is he?

Suddenly a name popped into Steve's mind. Oh, no, he thought. It couldn't be. Marcus Robard? That's crazy.

Marcus was the person he had seen in the *City Daily* building. I wonder why I should suddenly think of him? Steve asked himself.

"Steve, look!" Jim's voice cut into his thoughts. "The end of the tunnel!"

Steve's heart sprang with joy as he saw the narrow opening some hundred feet ahead. Where did it lead? What was beyond it? He wished now that he and his father had ventured deeper into the tunnel than they had that day his father wanted to write an article about it.

He shook with fear, nervousness, and with the cold of his damp clothes. Man, how long would he and Jim have to wear them before they could get into clean, dry ones? We could have pneumonia by then, he thought miserably. He couldn't shake the fear out of his mind.

They arrived at the mouth of the tunnel. Steve yanked on the reins, drawing Fire to a halt, as he saw looming in front of them the side of a tall building.

"The back of a barn," he whispered, recognizing its outline.

"Yeah. Do you know whose it is?" Jim whispered back.

"No. But I'm going to find out."

Steve swung his leg over the horse.

"Where you going?" Jim asked.

"Stay with Fire," said Steve, dropping

lightly to the ground. "And for crying out loud, shut off that flashlight!"

Jim snapped it off, leaving them in semidarkness.

"Let me have it," said Steve.

Jim gave it to him, and Steve took off toward the barn. It was about fifty feet beyond the mouth of the tunnel. The pale moon shining on it showed no windows on the side that faced him. But he saw a door. And it was closed.

Naturally, Steve thought. The headless rider wouldn't leave it open, would he? Not if he had gone through it.

Steve got to the door and hesitated. He suddenly felt very scared. This was probably the closest he had been to the headless rider.

Plucking up his courage, he grabbed the door latch, pushed it down and gently pulled the door open. Warm air gushed out at him as if from an oven. He smelled hay, and the acrid odor of manure.

He stood in the open doorway for a full five seconds before he realized how exposed he was. Anyone inside the barn could see his silhouette easily.

Quickly he took another step inside and

closed the door. He stood a while, looking around, trying to see into the dense shadows. His ears strained for a sound—the slightest sound.

Man, it's spooky, he thought. Why did I decide to come in here alone?

Well, because I didn't want to risk something drastic happening to Jim again, that's why, Steve told himself. Sure, Jim had said to go ahead. But deep inside he was still scared.

I admire him, Steve thought. He's got spunk.

He heard something skitter across the floor and froze. Was it a rat? Then he heard a loud squeak and ducked as something flew over his head. He flashed on the light and saw bats zooming in all directions under the high ceiling.

He shivered. He hated bats. He had always been frightened of them, although he wasn't sure why. He had read that it was a myth about bats getting into people's hair. Yet he wished they weren't around.

He saw bales of hay piled up in rows almost to the ceiling toward the opposite side of the barn. An old, rusted wagon wheel rested against one wall. A shiny-pointed bale hook

hung on a spike driven into a post.

Whose barn is this? Steve asked himself for the umpteenth time. Who has a farm at this end of the tunnel?

He tiptoed ahead. Although he tried not to make a sound, the floorboards squeaked under his weight.

He reached the end of a pile of bales, paused, and shone the light around the corner of it. Nothing. He tiptoed toward the other side of the barn where his light had barely reached.

He heard a sound behind him. Had a floorboard squeaked? Was someone following him? His skin felt as if spiders were crawling over him. He held his breath as he flashed the light behind him, held it there for a while.

Then he heard a snap. The door!

He raced down to the end of the bales of hay, down across the floor to the door. He reached it, grabbed the latch, depressed it and pushed.

Then he saw the padlock, higher up. Locked.

Nine

He vanished at will,
For midnight was his hour
To frolic.

STEVE TRIED again and again to force the door open. But it held fast.

Cold sweat popped out on his face. Suddenly he wasn't chilled anymore. And he felt almost dry. The barn was warm. It was smelly, but warm.

He stemmed an impulse to shout. Why shout? he thought. Even if Jim heard him, what could he do? He couldn't get in.

Steve shone the flashlight around the walls where he figured the headless rider might be lurking. Or running.

But he saw nothing.

His mind jumped back to his mother and father. To their warning remarks. He wished his father had come with him instead of Jim. His father might figure out a way to get out of this.

But, obviously, venturing into the night on a horse after a phantom rider wasn't his father's thing, Steve reminded himself. Years ago, when his father was younger, he might have relished an opportunity like this. Chasing hot news was in his father's blood.

But his father had mellowed over the years. He wasn't as well as he used to be. He depended on his reporters to bring in the news, hot or whatever.

Steve turned his back to the door. He shone the light straight ahead again, weaved it gently back and forth in an arc.

Once again Marcus Robard's name came to mind. Marcus' father owned at least half a dozen horses. And Marcus was an excellent rider.

Was it really Marcus on that horse? Was it Marcus impersonating the headless horseman? Why? Was it because David D. Davidson III had talked him into doing it? Was it because the greedy publisher could then have a sensational scoop that would help drive Steve's father out of the newspaper business? Would Marcus stoop as low as that?

But this wasn't the Robards' barn. Steve knew the Robards' barn inside and out. And it was located in another part of the county.

So where am I? Steve asked himself. Whose barn is this?

He heard a sound behind him. It came from outside. He listened.

"Steve!" Jim's voice. "Steve! Can you hear me?"

Steve rushed to the door. He slammed a fist against it.

"Jim! Yes, I can hear you! But the door's locked!"

But hope flared in him. Good old Jim. He had been getting impatient, worried. He had to come and see what was happening, Steve thought.

But what could Jim do now?

Hey, wait a minute! The rope! Steve thought. The rope they had brought along—just in case they needed it! Like now!

"Jim!" he called out.

"Yes?"

"Tie the rope to the door latch! Have Fire

pull the door open!"

"Right!" came Jim's voice. "Steady, Fire. Steady," Steve heard him say.

Steve waited patiently as he stood by the door. Suddenly another sound reached his ears. It came from inside the barn. A mixed kind of sound—something grating and squealing.

Steve tensed.

Then he heard Jim outside again, coaxing the horse to go ahead. A moment later the door squeaked and groaned as it began to bend outward.

All at once part of the casement gave way and the door snapped loose.

"You did it, Jim!" Steve ran out into the night. "And so did you, Fire, old girl!"

He removed the rope from the door latch, then quickly coiled it up again and replaced it on the saddle horn.

"He lock it on you?" Jim asked, wide-eyed, as Steve mounted Fire.

"Who else?" said Steve.

"Then you saw him?"

"No, I didn't. I was behind bales of hay when he locked it." Steve jabbed his heels against Fire's ribs. "Go, Fire," he ordered, and they rode into the building. Steve shone the flashlight straight ahead, then in a wide arc around them.

There was a flurry of flying creatures overhead.

"Hey! Bats!" Jim cried.

There were more now, Steve noticed, than when he had first entered the barn. They were flying around in what appeared to be haphazard courses, obviously disturbed by the noise the boys were making. But Steve knew of their built-in sonar system. He knew they wouldn't strike each other, or land smack against the walls as it seemed they might.

"Just ignore them," he said.

"Yeah, sure," replied Jim, unconvinced.

They rode in the direction Steve had walked earlier, then turned right, searched the floor and the corners. Nothing. Then they turned and headed in the opposite direction.

"This is spooky," Jim whispered.

Steve didn't answer. His entire attention was focused on any sound he might hear that could come from the strange rider.

As they approached the wall a long, snakelike object seemed to be hanging down on it, moving slowly to and fro.

Steve tugged gently on the reins, slowing up the horse and holding the flashlight more steadily on the object.

It was a rope dangling from the ceiling.

They moved closer to it. When they reached the rope, Steve shone the light upward and saw that it circled around a pulley and then down again to the top of a door, where it was tied in a knot to a large eye hook.

Now Steve knew how the headless horseman had disappeared.

He grabbed the end of the rope, pulled on it, and the door rose with a soft, grating sound. He realized that this was the sound he had heard earlier.

He flashed the light beyond the opened door and drew in his breath. A narrow path, like a tunnel, led down into the ground by way of a ramp.

What was down there? Steve wondered. Was it dangerous to venture any farther? More dangerous than it had been, that is?

Tension mounted in Steve as he paused to think it out.

Ten

His anger ignited like a torch
To destroy anyone who dared
To interfere.

"WHAT'RE YOU waiting for?" Jim whispered. "There's the hook for the rope. Fasten it and let's get moving."

Steve hesitated. Suppose they ventured down into that dungeonlike place and got locked in? Then what?

But the headless horseman had gone down there, hadn't he? And he had closed the door behind him. Would he close it if he knew there wasn't another way out?

"Okay," agreed Steve.

He saw that the end of the rope had been made into a loop. He shivered. It reminded him of a hangman's noose. *Like the one that had hanged Cyrus Cornfield?*

He looped the rope over the hook. It left the door scarcely high enough for them to pass under. Even Fire had to duck her head slightly to avoid hitting the door.

They descended the ramp, which was made of old railroad ties, and finally reached a flat, wood-plank floor. Flashing his light around, Steve saw right away what this place was.

A wine cellar.

The smell of wine was heavy in the cool air. A walkway led straight ahead. On both sides of it were large barrels perched on wooden racks. Each barrel had a spigot on it.

But there was no sign of anything else.

"You sure he came in here?" Jim asked.

"I'm sure I heard that overhead door open," Steve answered. "He must've come in here."

They rode toward the back end of the cellar.

Suddenly there was a loud, whinnying sound behind them. The thunder of pounding hooves.

"He's behind us!" Jim cried.

Terror gripped Steve. He reeled Fire around. At the sudden jolt in her ribs, the horse grunted and jerked her head as she turned around in the narrow area between the two rows of barrels.

"Go, Fire, go!" Steve urged, lowering his head like a jockey.

Up ahead of them they could see another horse, ridden by a horseman in a black costume, bounding up the ramp.

The horseman had no head.

Steve saw him pause beside the hook on to which the rope was looped. Saw him grab the rope and pull it free.

"Move, Fire!" Steve cried. He jabbed his heels harder into the horse's ribs.

Fire sped through the cellar and up the ramp just as the door began to descend.

"Duck!" Steve yelled, and lowered his head to avoid the descending door. They plunged through just in time, and heard the door strike the floor as it dropped behind them.

Steve shone the flashlight on the horseman, who wasn't more than ten feet ahead of them now. What a weird sight he was, Steve thought. Tall, wide-shouldered. *Headless.*

Is it you, Marcus? Is it really you in that weird-looking outfit? Steve wondered.

But the horse didn't look familiar. It didn't belong to the Robards. He was sure of that. He knew every one of the Robards' horses.

So who could . . . ?

The horseman was turning, riding his horse toward the broken door of the barn.

He's scared of us! Steve thought with sudden jubilation. He wants to get away so as not to be discovered!

"After him, Fire!" he coaxed. "Don't let him get away!"

The headless horseman raced out of the barn, Fire close behind him. Outside, where they had more room to maneuver, Fire inched up alongside the other animal.

"Stay with her, Jim!" Steve yelled as he leaned to the side and yielded the reins to his friend.

He started to reach over toward the headless horseman, but the rider pulled away from Steve, striking his own horse with a whip to make it go faster. The whip seemed to do some good, for the animal began to creep ahead.

"Faster, Fire! Faster!" Steve urged, digging his heels into the horse's ribs. He couldn't lose his target now!

Gradually Fire began to close the gap between her and the headless rider again. Steve

could hear her quick breaths, her hard, pounding hooves.

They were almost neck and neck—Fire and the other horse—and Steve was ready to jump. But just then the headless rider turned. His right hand swung around. His whip whirled in a short arc and slithered over Steve's head.

Steve ducked, his nerves screaming. If that whip had wrapped around his neck, he would have been a goner.

"Keep away from me! Keep away!" a high, shrieking cry came from within that flowing black robe.

So he can talk! Steve thought. Now, that's something for a man who hasn't got a head!

The horses were neck and neck, now. And the headless rider was once again whirling his whip over his head, ready to bring it around in a fast, bone-cracking snap. Maybe this time his aim would be more accurate!

Steve dove, striking the headless rider on his side and knocking him off his horse. Both went plunging to the ground, Steve rolling on top of the other rider, who felt as real and alive as Steve himself was.

"Hold it! Hold it!" that same shrieking voice

cried again. The costume fell off the phantom rider. "What do you want to do? Break every bone in my body?"

Steve's heart almost stopped. He stared at a moonlit, pale, slightly wrinkled face.

"Grandpa!" he cried, stunned, flabbergasted. "Grandpa George!"

Eleven

In anguish he yielded:
Embarrassed,
Yet proud.

"I DON'T believe this, Grandpa," Steve exclaimed, staring wide-eyed at his grandfather. "You, of all people!"

"Yes, me. Surprised, aren't you?" Grandpa George rose to his feet. He was breathing hard, gasping for breath. Steve gave him a hand and helped him brush the dirt off his pants.

"You almost got me with that whip, Grandpa!" Steve said.

"Bah! I missed you on purpose," the old man snorted. "I wanted to scare you. But you don't scare easily, do you?" He bent over and started to roll the black costume up into a ball.

Steve heard him chuckle and saw a quick smile cross his face.

"But why, Grandpa?" he asked. "Why did you do it?"

"For your father," Grandpa George said, straightening up, the pile of clothes in his arms. "For his newspaper, what do you think?"

"But the *City Daily* scooped you, sir," Jim broke in. "They're the ones who printed the news of seeing the headless horseman."

"I know, I know," Grandpa George muttered, disgruntled. "But I had to try something. I couldn't stand by and see my son's newspaper dying a slow death. I thought that this—this business of bringing the legend of the headless horseman to life—would be a scoop for him, because I would ride past his house. And I knew you two boys would still be out there, fishing. That you'd see me ride by and tell your father."

"We did exactly that, Grandpa," Steve said, his heart suddenly going out to his grandfather for the trouble he had gone through. "But neither Dad nor Mom believed us. Otherwise—"

"Otherwise it would have been a scoop for him," Grandpa George interrupted. "I know. But other people saw me and told Davidson. He realized how hot that item could be against your father and used it." He sighed. "Oh, well. Call my horse. I'm tired. You boys gave me the ride of my life and my bones are screaming."

Steve grinned. "You gave us quite a ride, too, Grandpa. You're really a great guy, Grandpa George," he said.

"Sure, I am. Call my horse."

"First, tell me—whose barn is that with the wine barrels in the cellar?"

"It belongs to an old friend of mine," Grandpa answered. "But he hasn't used either the barn or the wine cellar in ages. Come to think of it, you'll have to fix that door."

"Yes, I'll do that," Steve promised.

Then he called out to Grandpa's horse. It ambled forward, and he helped his grandfather mount, although he knew the old man could do it without his help. Then he and Jim climbed up on Fire and followed Grandpa George home.

The next day the *Courier* carried an article and an assortment of photographs. Steve's film had survived its dunking! There was Grandpa George in his headless horseman's costume. The article told about his rides the past two nights. Steve's father had written the article and had it printed on the front page.

"The truth," he said, "had to be told, and let the chips fall where they may."

That afternoon the phone in the Russell household rang three times before Jim, the closest, answered it.

"Just a minute," he said into the phone and looked at Steve. "It's for you," he said. "It's your dad."

Steve's heart pounded. He had hardly slept that morning. Nothing else was on his mind except what had happened last night and very early this morning, and what the effects would be of that article and those pictures.

Oh, Grandpa George! he had thought so many times since he had seen the costume fall off his grandfather's shoulders. You surely pulled the caper of the century. I just hope that Cyrus Cornfield in his grave won't get mad and come back to haunt you!

He took the phone from Jim. "Yes, Dad?"

"Son! Have I got good news!" his father cried excitedly. "My phone's been blasting like crazy ever since the newspaper hit the streets!"

Steve's eyes began to cloud. "What's the news, Dad?"

"The edition's all sold out! We're printing more copies! And all my advertisers are pleased! They're laughing about that 'scoop' in Davidson's *City Daily*! We're going to get back in the black, son! We've stopped Davidson for a while! Thanks to you, to Jim, and to Grandpa George!" He paused, and Steve could hear him trying to catch his breath. "By the way, is your grandfather there? I'd like to speak to him."

"He sure is," Steve said. Proud tears burning in his throat, he held the receiver out to his grandfather. "He wants to talk to you, Grandpa," he said.

About the Author

MATT CHRISTOPHER has been writing since he was fourteen years old. The oldest of nine children, Mr. Christopher graduated from school in Ludlowville, New York, where he played baseball and football. After graduating, he played basketball and semipro baseball.

During the years leading to full-time writing, he worked at many jobs while continuing to write, strengthening his craft. During these years he wrote 175 short stories and articles, a comic-strip series, a detective story, and a play.

Now with more than 30 books in print, Mr. Christopher has written THE RETURN OF THE HEADLESS HORSEMAN, the kind of mystery he enjoys reading.

Matt Christopher lives and writes in Rock Hill, South Carolina.

Cates:
Taylor